This book belongs to
-------------------------------------------------------------------

Copyright © 2024 Kate Pricklewood
All rights reserved.
ISBN: 978-1-0685583-3-7

# The Hedgehog Family's Berry Bonanza

## Kate Pricklewood

Once upon a time, in their cozy burrow on the edge of the great forest, lived a very prickly, very curious, and very adventurous family of hedgehogs.

There was Daddy Hedgehog, who was strong, wise, and always losing things in his *prickly coat* (one time he found a spoon in there!); Mommy Hedgehog, who was kind, caring, and could bake the fluffiest nut bread (seriously, it was so fluffy it might just float away); and their three children — Holly, Henry, and Hazel — who were always asking questions like, "Why don't fish have feet?" and "Can a butterfly burp?"

One sunny morning, as the birds sang outside their burrow, the hedgehog family decided it was the perfect day for... drumroll please... a berry hunt!
Mommy Hedgehog gave everyone a small basket and said, "Let's see who can collect the most berries! But remember, no eating them until we get back home!"

"Challenge accepted!" said Holly, grinning.
"I'm going to find ALL the berries!" Henry said, puffing out his chest.
"I'm going to EAT all the berries — oh wait, no, collect, I meant collect" Hazel giggled.

The hedgehog family waddled off into the forest, their noses twitching with excitement. The trees were filled with sunlight, the leaves rustling gently, and the forest floor was sprinkled with patches of juicy berries.

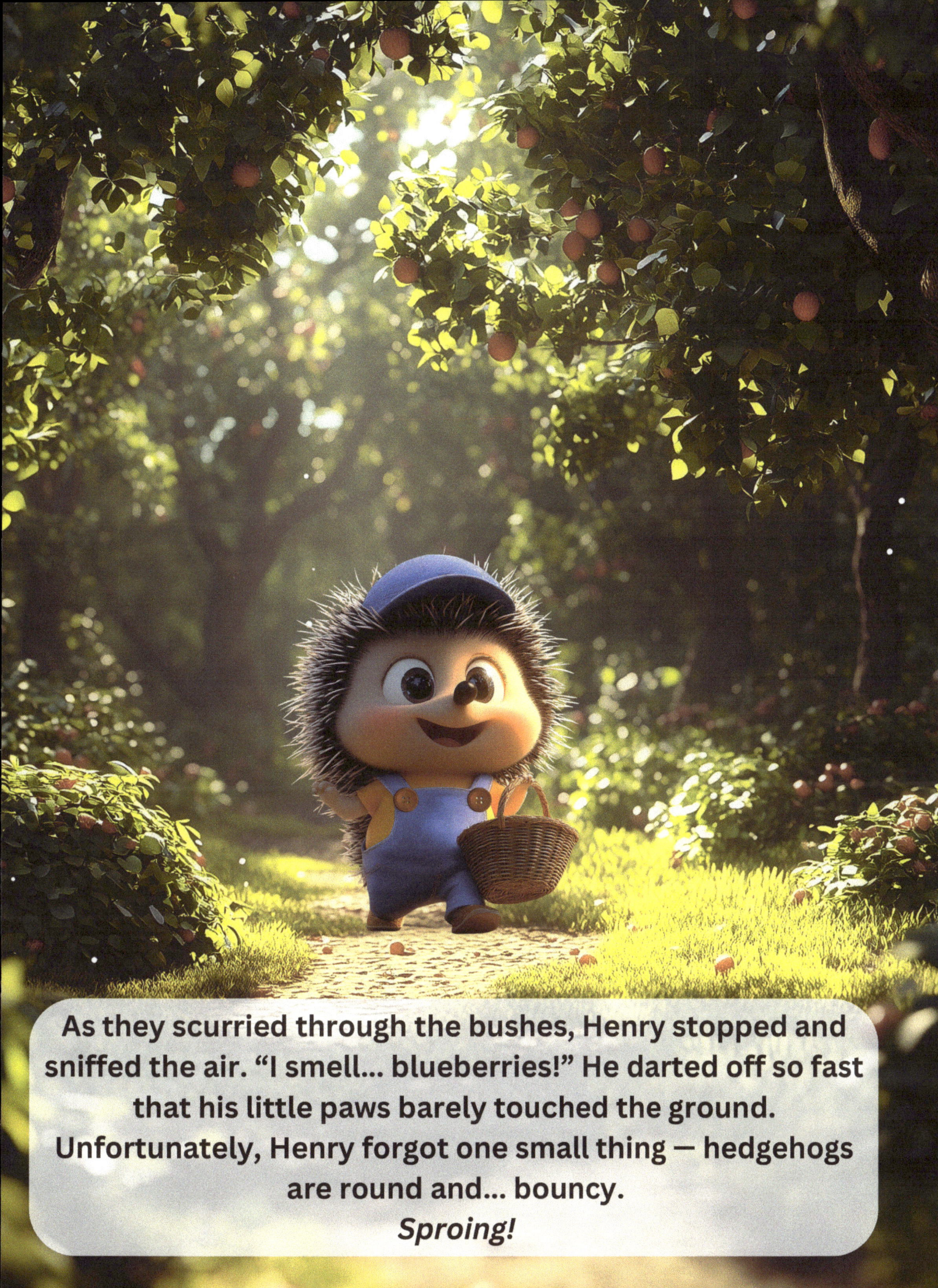

As they scurried through the bushes, Henry stopped and sniffed the air. "I smell... blueberries!" He darted off so fast that his little paws barely touched the ground. Unfortunately, Henry forgot one small thing — hedgehogs are round and... bouncy.
*Sproing!*

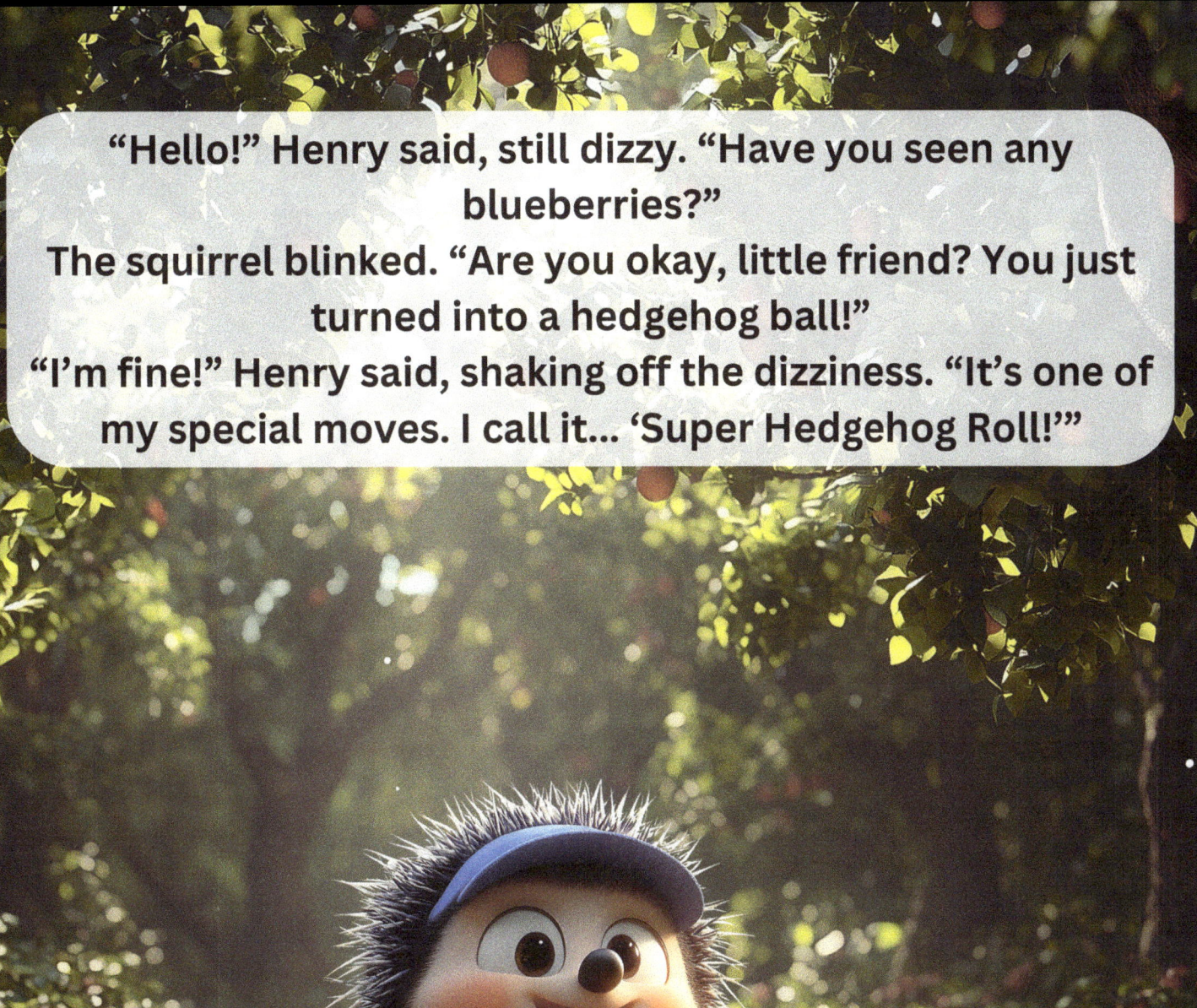

"Hello!" Henry said, still dizzy. "Have you seen any blueberries?"
The squirrel blinked. "Are you okay, little friend? You just turned into a hedgehog ball!"
"I'm fine!" Henry said, shaking off the dizziness. "It's one of my special moves. I call it... 'Super Hedgehog Roll!'"

The squirrel giggled. "Well, Super Hedgehog, the blueberries are right behind you!"

Henry spun around and there they were — plump, juicy blueberries just waiting to be picked. He joyfully filled his basket and gave the squirrel a cheerful wave. "Mission accomplished!"

Meanwhile, Holly was off in another part of the forest, carefully picking strawberries. She was very serious about it, inspecting each one like a berry detective. "Too squishy... too small... ah, perfect!" She plucked a perfect strawberry and dropped it into her basket.

Suddenly, she heard a flutter of wings. Holly looked up to see a butterfly fluttering around her head.
"Hey there!" Holly smiled. "You wouldn't happen to know where the best strawberries are, would you?"
The butterfly landed gently on Holly's nose and flapped its wings.
"Well, I guess that's a no" Holly said with a giggle. "But I will follow you anyway!"

The butterfly led her to a little sunny patch where the biggest, juiciest strawberries were growing. Holly gasped in delight. "You are the best berry-hunting partner ever!" she called after the butterfly as it flew away.

Meanwhile, Hazel was having a bit of a different adventure. She wasn't exactly the best at sticking to the "no eating until we get home" rule. As soon as she found a raspberry bush, she popped a berry into her mouth.
"Mmmm... this is delicious!" she said, happily munching away.

Then, she heard a little rustle in the bushes. Hazel turned and saw two rabbits staring at her, their little noses twitching curiously.
"Hi!" Hazel said, her mouth still full of raspberry. "Want some berries?"
The rabbits hopped closer and tilted their heads.

"Okay, but only if you promise not to tell Mommy Hedgehog" Hazel whispered. She held out some raspberries, and the rabbits nibbled them happily.
One of the rabbits twitched its nose and gave Hazel a wink.
"Don't worry, your secret is safe with us!"

By lunchtime, the hedgehog family met back in the forest clearing, their baskets full of berries. Holly had strawberries, Henry had blueberries, and Hazel... well, Hazel had some raspberries and a very large raspberry-stained smile. Daddy Hedgehog chuckled. "Looks like someone's been having a sneaky snack attack!"

They all laughed and began waddling home together. But just as they were nearing the burrow, Daddy Hedgehog suddenly stopped and gasped.
"Oh no!" he exclaimed. "I've lost my basket! I must have dropped it somewhere along the way!"

Holly and Henry giggled. "Don't worry Daddy" Holly said, "you always lose something!"

Henry grinned. "Last time, it was your hat, remember? And we found it on your own head!"

Daddy Hedgehog sighed dramatically. "Ah, the challenges of being a hedgehog. Too many prickles and not enough pockets!"

But just then, a little bird swooped down and chirped happily, dropping Daddy Hedgehog's basket right next to him.

"Thanks!" Daddy Hedgehog said with a smile. "I guess it's good to have friends with wings when you've got no pockets!"

"Well, I might be the best at losing things" said Daddy "but at least I haven't lost my sense of direction. Wait... hold on... is home this way, or... that way?"
The whole family burst into laughter.
"Good thing Mommy is here to keep us on track" Mommy Hedgehog said with a playful grin, pointing ahead. "Otherwise, we would be stuck circling the berry bushes for days!"

Back at their cozy burrow, the family sat down for a berry feast. They had berry sandwiches, berry juice, and of course, Mommy Hedgehog's famous nut bread.
As they ate, they laughed about their berry-filled adventure.

"We are the best berry hunters in the whole forest!" Holly said proudly.
"And the best berry snackers!" Hazel added with a wink.
Henry puffed out his chest. "And I am the fastest berry collector — just ask the squirrel I surprised!"

Daddy Hedgehog grinned. "Well, I am the world champion of... losing baskets! I should get a medal — if I can find that too!"
They all laughed together, feeling full and happy.

And that night, as they snuggled up in their cozy burrow, they dreamed of their next adventure — because with a family as prickly, playful and loving as theirs, there were always more adventures just around the corner.

## Daddy Hedgehog

*Strong, wise, and always misplacing things, Daddy Hedgehog is full of love for his family. With a sense of humor as big as his prickly coat, he adds fun to every adventure, even if he loses his basket along the way!*

## Mommy Hedgehog

*Caring, thoughtful, and a master of baking, Mommy Hedgehog is the heart of the family. Whether she is making the fluffiest nut bread or keeping the family on track, her kindness shines through every moment.*

## Holly
*Curious and clever, Holly is always asking questions and loves being precise in everything she does. She is the family's strawberry expert, picking only the very best with the help of a fluttery friend.*

## Henry
*Full of energy and adventure, Henry is always on the move! With his "Super Hedgehog Roll," he turns any mishap into a fun moment, especially when he discovers a patch of blueberries in the funniest way.*

## Hazel
*Playful and cheeky, Hazel loves berries — especially eating them! Always sneaking a taste when she thinks no one's watching, she brings laughter to the group with her sweet, mischievous nature.*